Hairdo!

What We Do and Did to Our Hair

BY RUTH FREEMAN SWAIN

ILLUSTRATED BY CAT BOWMAN SMITH

Holiday House / NEW YORK

For my parents and Lisa:
straight, wavy, and naturally curly
—R. F. S.

To Mindy
—C. B. S.

Printed in the United States of America
www.holidayhouse.com
The text typeface is Rotation.
The artwork for this book was created in gouache.
First Edition

Library of Congress Cataloging-in-Publication Data
Swain, Ruth Freeman.
Hairdo!: what we do and did to our hair / by Ruth Freeman Swain;
illustrated by Cat Bowman Smith.—1st ed.
p. cm.
Includes bibliographical references.
Summary: Depicts how people have viewed, worn, and
changed their hairstyles throughout history and in various cultures.
ISBN 0-8234-1522-8
1. Hairstyles—History—Juvenile literature. [1. Hairstyles—History.]
I. Smith, Cat Bowman, ill. II. Title.
GT2290 .S9 2001
391.5—dc21   99-013350

You may have been born with Grandpa's teeth, with Aunt Edith's ears, or with Daddy's dimple. You inherited your type of hair from your family, too. BUT, aren't you glad you didn't inherit their hairdos?

The best things about hair are: it grows and it is so easy to change.

Ancient Egyptian men preferred to shave their heads and wear elaborate wigs. Women sometimes wore their own hair and sometimes wore wigs over their hair.

At evening parties, special guests were given cones of perfumed beeswax to put on top of their heads. As the hot night wore on, the wax melted and slowly oozed over their hair. The melting wax was supposed to cool the person underneath.

Egyptians were horrified by "those hairy Greeks," as they called them. The Greeks began to shave only when Alexander the Great ordered his soldiers to cut off their beards. In battle, beards gave the enemy something easy to grab. At first, older Greek men thought shaving was terrible, but it soon became the fashion for everyone.

While Roman men visited their local barbershop every morning, Roman women had their hair piled into towers of curls by servants at home. Sprinkles of gold dust and blond hairpieces made of hair taken from German captives were popular. Keeping up with the latest fashion was so important that one fine lady had her marble bust carved with a removable stone hairdo so new styles could be added and she'd never look out of date.

On a winter night in sixteenth-century France, King Francis I surprised a friend of his with a snowball fight. During the fight, Francis was hit on the head by a torch and badly burned. Doctors had to cut his hair to treat his wounds.

To keep him company, the king's friends decided to cut their hair, too. And when Francis grew a beard to hide his scars, they did the same. Hearing of the new French hairstyle, King Henry VIII of England, who liked being fashionable, ordered haircuts for everyone at the English court.

When Louis XIV put on a wig to hide his thinning hair, wigs became the fashion for all men, whether they were growing bald or not, in seventeenth-century France.

THE CAMPAIGN WIG

THE SUNDAY BUCKLE OR MAJOR BOB

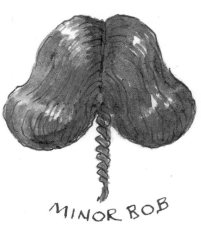

MINOR BOB

THE NATURAL

To make all these wigs, wig makers
first cleaned and rolled hair around clay curling pins.
Women's hair was supposed to be the strongest. The wrapped pins were
boiled for three hours, then taken to a bakery and baked inside
loaves of bread! Moisture and heat from the bread made the hair strong and
flexible. After more combing and sorting, the hair was sewn onto
a skullcap, trimmed, and curled, and the wig was ready
for the man or boy who had ordered it.

RAMILLIE WIG

THE BAG WIG

THE BRIGADIER

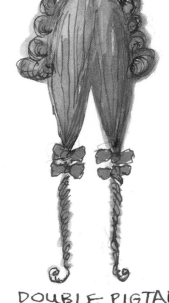

DOUBLE PIGTAIL

Women's hairstyles in eighteenth-century Europe rose to towering headdresses more than 2 feet high. Structures of wire and false hair were built on a woman's head, coated with lard that dried rock hard, and dusted with flour. The whole thing was left in place for weeks or months. That left plenty of time for bugs and small animals to move in and make themselves at home.

Hair made a terrible stink as the lard turned rancid, and the only way to scratch was with long scratchers that looked like knitting needles. Headdresses were decorated with everything from feathers to fruit, a tiny coach and horses to a miniature sea battle. But these hairdos were the latest fashion and to be fashionable was all that mattered.

Many Native Americans believed that hair had special powers. Any hair combed from a head was burned. This way an enemy couldn't find the hair and gain power over that person.

Native Americans wore the hairstyle of their tribe. Iroquois men cut their hair very short on the sides, leaving a center ridge that they often decorated with feathers or deer hair.

Unmarried Hopi girls dressed their hair in two big bunches called squash blossoms, one above each ear. When they wed, they wore a braid down the back instead.

When the Manchus invaded China in 1644, they ordered every man to shave the front of his head and wear a pigtail. There were fierce rebellions against the new rule. In time, however, the pigtail, or queue, which is a French word meaning "tail," became accepted.

Later, when many Chinese came to the United States to work, they were proud of their queues and continued to wear them. Some Americans were not kind to the Chinese. In the 1870s, San Francisco officials passed the Queue Ordinance, which called for queues of any Chinese arrested to be cut off. But a few years later, a judge declared that officials could not cut anyone's hair and the Queue Ordinance was stopped.

When Abraham Lincoln was running for president in 1860, he received this letter:

Dear Sir,

I am a little girl 11 years old, but want you should be President of the United States very much... I have got four brothers and part of them will vote for you any way, and if you will let your whiskers grow I will try to get the rest of them to vote for you. You would look a great deal better for your face is so thin.

Grace Bedell
Westfield, N.Y.

Abraham Lincoln did grow a beard, just as we see on our pennies today. Maybe he grew it because beards were very popular, maybe he grew it because a beard might make him look kind and wise to voters, and maybe he grew it because of a young girl's letter.

For centuries women had worn long hair. But in the early 1900s, they began to cut it off. This was unheard of. Women were walking into barbershops and asking barbers to bob their hair. Cut just below the ear, the bob was hard for many people to get used to.

Short hair made it possible for all women, rich and poor, old and young, to keep up with the latest fashion. Short hair was easier to care for, which was helpful to the growing number of women working outside the home. Short hair also allowed you to look just like your favorite movie star.

In Africa, traditional hairstyles indicate a person's tribe or cultural group. Teenage girls of the Himbas tribe in Namibia and Angola shave the front of their heads and braid the rest of their hair with plant fibers to make foot-long braids. When they marry, they add locks of hair from their brothers and husbands to their hairdos.

Masai girls and women in Tanzania and Kenya shave their heads and wear beaded headbands. When a Masai boy becomes a young warrior, his hair is braided, coated with red earth, and tied up in an elaborate hairstyle. These hairstyles are still worn today, though many Africans have chosen more western, less traditional styles.

During the 1960s, when many students, young people, and African Americans demanded more civil rights and changes in government policy, hair became the most obvious sign of protest. Students and hippies, both men and women, wore their hair long. African Americans, proud of their African heritage, wore their hair in Afros.

These natural hairstyles were very different from men's short, military-style crew cuts and women's puffed-up, or "bouffant," hairstyles of the time. A person's hair could show what they believed in, what they cared about, and probably what music they listened to.

Look at all the different hairstyles today: ponytails and pigtails, curls and coils, braids and bowls, and no hair at all. We can have long, straight hair in the morning and short, curly hair by afternoon, in any color we want.

Hairdos have always shown a lot about who we are. Some hairdos show what a person does, such as the legal wigs male and female barristers wear in English courts. Some hairdos show what a person believes, such as the curled side locks Orthodox Jews wear. Some hairdos show who we would like to be. A hairdo can impress one person and annoy the next.

The wonderful thing about hair is we can do it, and do it again, and no matter what we do, it will keep on growing, and growing, and growing.
So which "do" is you?

Hairy Information

The longest beard on record belonged to an Iowa farmer. When Hans Langseth died in 1927, his beard was $17^{1}/2$ feet long, dark at one end, white at the other. He wore his beard rolled around a corncob stuck into the bib of his overalls.

In fairy tales, Rapunzel, of course, had the longest (and strongest) hair. In real life, a woman in Massachusetts had hair 12 feet 2 inches long.

Hair grows about half an inch a month and, if left uncut, will usually grow 2 to 3 feet in length. Seasons, age, diet, and health affect hair growth; cutting hair does not. All mammals have hair, which gives them protection from cold, heat, and rain. As they evolved in the hot African climate, humans lost the thick fur on their bodies so they could perspire and cool themselves more efficiently.

Hair remains on our bodies today, but most of it is fine and almost invisible. The hair on our scalps is thicker to protect our heads from the sun and to cut down on heat loss in winter.

Hairs grow out of little pockets in our skin called follicles. Each follicle has a tiny oil gland and muscle attached to it. Oil coats the hair and keeps it soft. When the muscle contracts due to cold or fear, it is "hair raising" and gives us a "goose bump." This reflex may have been used for defense. If fur stands up, it makes an animal look bigger and fiercer. Goose bumps may also have been for protection from cold, since fur that is standing up holds more heat.

KERATIN: A protein that forms to harden...
fingernails,
animal claws,
reptile scales,
bird's feathers,
and human hair.

Brrr...I've got goose bumps!

Don't you wish!

As hair cells in the base of the follicle multiply and are pushed upward, they form a hard protein called keratin. Keratin is the same protein in fingernails, animal claws, reptile scales, and bird's feathers. Since hair is made of layers of dead cells, we can cut our hair without feeling a thing.

There are about 100,000 hairs on each of our heads. Some people may have as many as 150,000. A hair will grow for two to six years, then rest for about three months. During the next growing period, a new hair will push out the old one and the cycle begins again. We shed 50 to a 100 hair. When melanin stops being produced, a person's hair will be white. Baldness is also inherited, though hair loss can be caused by stress, illness, hormonal changes after childbirth, and treatments such as radiation. More men lose their hair than women. Some men like being bald; others don't.

To have healthy hair, eating the right foods and getting enough sleep and exercise are important. Hair should be washed regularly. Brushing and combing remove tangles, dust, and dirt, and spread the scalp's natural oils through the hair.

Ewww...gross!

hairs every day. Fortunately, hairs are shed at different times, not all at once!

Hair color and texture are inherited, with dark hair more common than blond. Melanin is the dark pigment that gives color to our hair and skin. With only a little melanin, a person will have blond or red

MELANIN: The pigment that gives color to our hair and skin.

Helpful Sources

Badt, Karin Luisa. *Hair There and Everywhere* (A World of Difference series). Chicago: Children's Press, 1994.

Cooper, Wendy. *Hair: Sex, Society, Symbolism.* New York: Stein and Day, 1971.

Fisher, Leonard Everett. *The Wigmakers* (Colonial American Craftsmen series). New York: Franklin Watts, Inc., 1965.

Severn, Bill. *The Long and Short of It: Five Thousand Years of Fun and Fury Over Hair.* New York: David McKay Co., 1971.

Tortora, Phyllis, and Keith Eubank. *A Survey of Historic Costume.* New York: Fairchild Publications, 1989.

7/05   3   6/05

4/12   3   6/05
1-16   3   ———
3/17   3   ———
2/21   3   8/05
11/22   3   8/05
5/24   3   6/05

BAKER & TAYLOR